IMAGINE THAT

Licensed exclusively to Imagine That Publishing Ltd
Tide Mill Way, Woodbridge, Suffolk, IP12 1AP, UK
www.imaginethat.com
Copyright © 2020 Imagine That Group Ltd
All rights reserved
0 2 4 6 8 9 7 5 3 1
Manufactured in China

Written by Sarah Lucy
Illustrated by Lucy Barnard

ISBN 978-1-78958-583-4

A catalogue record for this book is available from the British Library

For Charlie and Freddie, the sweetest of all treats.

The TREATS Tree

Written by Sarah Lucy
Illustrated by Lucy Barnard

It was soon going to be Big Squirrel's birthday, and his friends and family were busy getting ready for his surprise party.

'We need your help, Little Squirrel!'
said Wise Owl. 'The party is only a few
days away and there's lots to do.'

'Your job is picking lots of delicious berries for everyone to eat,' said Wise Owl, handing Little Squirrel a big basket.

Little Squirrel let out a sigh. 'Hunting for berries is boring!' he thought.

The truth was, Little Squirrel was a little bit lazy.

'I'd much rather play,' Little Squirrel said to himself.
Then he scampered off into the forest, playing with
his basket as he went.

After lots of playing and no berry-picking,
Little Squirrel stopped for a rest.

Just then, he spotted the strangest tree he had ever seen. Hanging from its branches were striped peppermint candy canes.

'I am quite hungry,' said Little Squirrel,
lifting down a delicious candy cane.

'But there isn't enough for everyone, so I'll keep this tree a secret,' he said, as he headed for home.

The next day, Little Squirrel was meant to pick delicious berries for Big Squirrel's party, but instead he scampered straight to the magical treats tree.

This time there were frosted cupcakes hanging from its branches!

'These cupcakes look delicious,' cried Little Squirrel, licking his lips. 'I am quite hungry – and they are too small to share!'

And with that, Little Squirrel gobbled up all of the cupcakes!
But he didn't pick a single berry.

The next day was the same. When Little Squirrel left to pick berries, he scampered straight to the magical treats tree and found new tasty treats waiting for him.

Once again, Little Squirrel ate the treats all by himself!
And just like yesterday, he forgot all about the berries.

On the morning of Big Squirrel's surprise party, Little Squirrel scampered through the forest to the magical treats tree. This time, he found yummy blueberry muffins hanging from its branches.

Just then, a mummy bird appeared with her hungry babies, looking for something to eat.

The mummy bird flapped her wings and pecked at the berry bushes. She picked the biggest, juiciest berries she could find and popped them into her babies' mouths one by one.

'That looks like hard work,'
thought Little Squirrel.

But the mummy bird didn't stop there.
Her babies were very hungry and she
had to pick lots and lots of berries.

As Little Squirrel watched, he felt sad.
All this time he had been thinking about
himself – not Big Squirrel's surprise party.
Suddenly, his muffins didn't taste so yummy.
It was time to do the right thing.

Back in the woodland clearing, Big Squirrel's surprise birthday party was about to start.

But someone was missing …

'Little Squirrel!' all the animals cried as Little Squirrel appeared,
his basket overflowing with big juicy berries.

'Sorry I'm late!' said Little Squirrel with a big smile on his face. 'I've brought lots of berries for you all!' The happy animals gathered around and tucked into the juicy berries. Little Squirrel watched his smiling friends.

'Tomorrow I'll take everyone to the treats tree for a very special surprise,' thought Little Squirrel. 'Sharing is the sweetest treat of all!'